Sammy's Boat Ride

AuthorHouse™
1663 Liberty Drive
Bloomington, IN 47403
www.authorhouse.com
Phone: 833-262-8899

This is a work of fiction. All of the characters, names, incidents, organizations, and dialogue in this novel are either the products of the author's imagination or are used fictitiously.

Because of the dynamic nature of the Internet, any web addresses or links contained in this book may have changed since publication and may no longer be valid. The views expressed in this work are solely those of the author and do not necessarily reflect the views of the publisher, and the publisher hereby disclaims any responsibility for them.

Any people depicted in stock imagery provided by Getty Images are models, and such images are being used for illustrative purposes only.
Certain stock imagery © Getty Images.

This book is printed on acid-free paper.

ISBN: 978-1-4520-1702-0 (sc)

Library of Congress Control Number: 2010905880

Print information available on the last page.

Published by AuthorHouse 10/29/2020

Sammy lived in Eddies house.

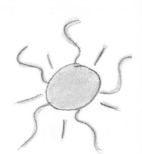

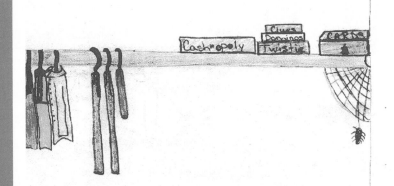

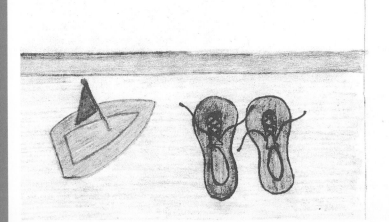

Sammy was a Spider. He stayed in Eddie's closet. In that closet Eddie kept a small boat.

Sammy used it for a bed.

He was a happy spider aboard the boat

Eddie walked to the lake.
He put the boat in the water
and started to play.

Sammy woke up and saw the boat was in the water.

He got scared because he could not swim.

Sammy tried to run to Eddie for help, but Eddie was afraid of spiders. He ran away leaving the boat in the water.

Sammy was trapped on the boat as it sailed farther from land. He was all alone, so he cried for help.

"I can help you," said a deep voice. It was Tom the fish. He wanted to eat Sammy n̲o̲t help him

"I can not see you." Called Sammy
"I am right here." Answered Tom
"Right where?" Asked Sammy

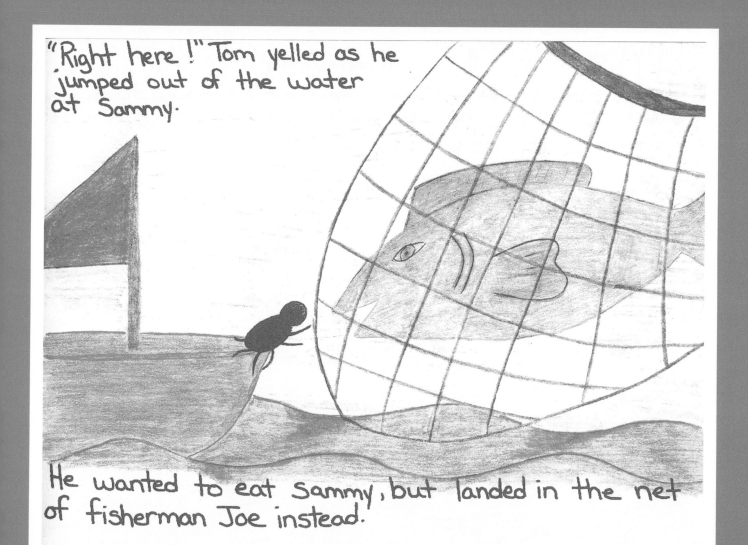

"Right here!" Tom yelled as he jumped out of the water at Sammy.

He wanted to eat Sammy, but landed in the net of fisherman Joe instead.

"Wow!" Said Joe, "A fish jumped into my net!"
Then Joe had an idea, he tied the small boat to the
end of his fishing pole. Sammy cried for help again an
another fish answered.

This fish was even bigger than Tom. Sammy was so afraid. The fish swam around the boat, and said "I am going to eat you!"

He jumped at Sammy, but fisherman Joe caught him in the net. "Wow-wee!" said Joe, "This is fun!" He started pulling the boat back and fourth to catch more fish.

"Help! Help!" Sammy yelled again and again. Fish were jumping everywhere trying to eat him, but landing in fisherman Joe's net. One big fish bit the line in half and the boat floated away.

Sammy kept quiet so the fish would not jump. Now the boat was getting closer to shore and Sammy hoped he could go home. Two boys on the shore saw the boat and raced towards it.

Sammy thought he was rescued. He was happy. When the boys saw Sammy they started to throw stones at him.

The noise woke up Mr. Snake and made him angry. He chased the two boys away, then he went to look at the boat.

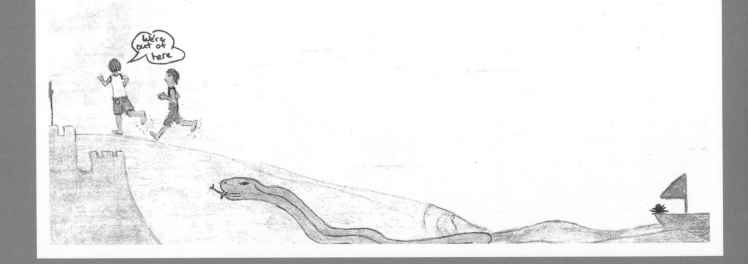

"Who's there?" asked Mr. Snake. "Only me." said Sammy. While he looked at Mr. Snake's head, Mr. Snakes tail was sneaking up behind Sammy to grab him. The tail came closer and closer. Mr. Snake then quickly swung his tail.

Luckily, Sammy sneezed and fell down. The tail missed Sammy and hit the boat instead, which pushed it all the way to the shore.

Just as Sammy was going to jump out of the boat and run for his life, a big hand scooped up the boat. Sammy saw that it was Eddie's mom.

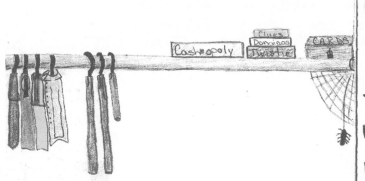

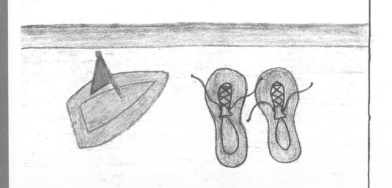

"Here's Eddie's boat", she said. Eddie's mom brought the boat home and put it in the closet. Sammy was happy. He was home at last!

The End

Printed in the United States
By Bookmasters